creation

cynthia rylant

BEACH LANE BOOKS

New York London Toronto Sydney New Delhi

In the beginning

God created the heaven and the earth.

And the earth was without form and void
   and darkness was upon the face
   of the deep.
And the spirit of God moved over the waters
   and God said, Let there be light.

And there was light.

And God saw the light,
that it was good.
And God divided the light
from the darkness.
And God called the light Day

and the darkness he called Night.

God said, Let the waters under the heaven
be gathered together unto one place,
and let the dry land appear.

And God called the dry land Earth
and the waters he called Seas.

And God saw that it was good.

And God said, Let the earth bring forth grass,

and the fruit tree yielding fruit,
whose seed is in itself: and it was so.

God made two great lights,
the greater light to rule the day

and the lesser light to rule the night.

He made the stars also.
And God set them in the firmament
of the heaven
to give light upon the earth.

And God created the great whales.
God blessed them, saying, Be fruitful and multiply
and fill the waters in the seas.

God created every living creature that moved:

od created every living creature that moved:

the beasts

the birds

and the creeping things.

And it was good.

God then made man and woman
and God said to them,
Replenish the earth
so that everything may multiply
and be fruitful.

He blessed them, these two who were most like him.

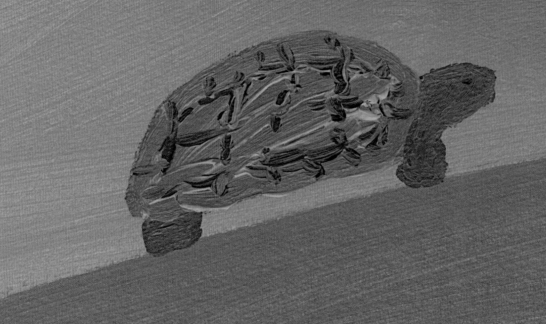

And when the evening and the morning
of the sixth day had passed,

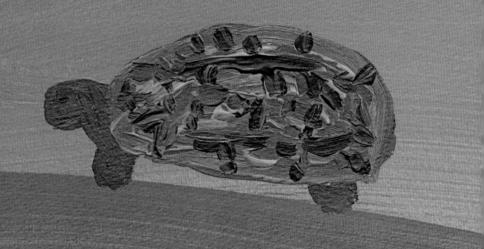

God was done with his work.

He looked at everything he had created and made, and behold, it was very good.

So, on the seventh day . . .

he rested.

BEACH LANE BOOKS
An imprint of Simon & Schuster Children's Publishing Division
1230 Avenue of the Americas, New York, New York 10020
Copyright © 2016 by Cynthia Rylant
The text for this book was adapted from chapters one and two
of the book of Genesis from the King James Version of the
Holy Bible.
BEACH LANE BOOKS is a trademark of Simon & Schuster, Inc.
For information about special discounts for bulk purchases, please
contact Simon & Schuster Special Sales at 1-866-506-1949 or
business@simonandschuster.com.
The Simon & Schuster Speakers Bureau can bring authors to
your live event. For more information or to book an event, contact
the Simon & Schuster Speakers Bureau at 1-866-248-3049 or visit
our website at www.simonspeakers.com.
For HC
Book design by Ann Bobco
The text for this book was set in PencilPete FONT.
The illustrations for this book were rendered in acrylic paint on
Bee Paper 100% rag, 90-pound cold-press watercolor paper.
Manufactured in China
0716 SCP
First Edition
10 9 8 7 6 5 4 3 2 1
CIP data for this book is available from the Library of Congress.
ISBN 9781481470391
ISBN 9781481470407 (eBook)